For William and William

Special thanks to Jen Arena and Valerie Navarro

Vivian the Dog Moves to the Big City
Copyright © 2017 by Mitch Boyer
All rights reserved. Manufactured in China.

Library of Congress Control Number: 2017934811

ISBN 978-0-06-267327-5

The artist used Capture One and Photoshop to create the photo illustrations for this book.
Typography by Chelsea C. Donaldson
17 18 19 20 21 SCP 10 9 8 7 6 5 4 3 2 1

First Edition

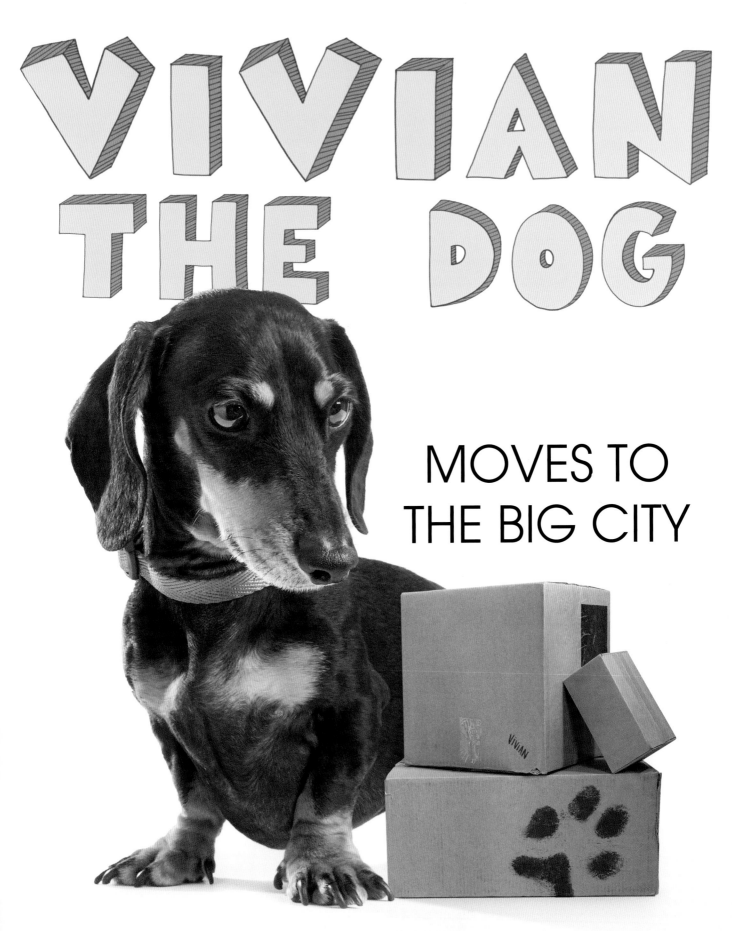

VIVIAN THE DOG

MOVES TO THE BIG CITY

MITCH BOYER

HARPER

An Imprint of HarperCollinsPublishers

Have you ever seen a dog like me before?

No? I didn't think so!

My name is Vivian, and this is where I live. Isn't it great? I love my big, open sky and big places to run!

But I'm moving somewhere even better . . .

the BIG CITY!

My humans pack a truck with boxes.

"Don't forget my favorite toy, please!"

The big city sounds like the perfect place for a big dog like me.

"Are we there yet?"

After a long trip, we're finally here.

wait, *this* is the big city?

It feels . . . small.

I can barely see the sky. My yard is a square of grass.
And the dogs? Tiny!

Like that one, walking past. That's my new neighbor Lulu.
She's lived here since she was a puppy.

"Lulu, what's up with this place? It's not so great. Why is it even called the big city?"

"Why?" she says. "Vivian, it's as plain as the nose on your face. Follow me. You'll fit right in here!"

I jump the fence and run after her. For a little dog, she's speedy!

"Look at this bridge. Do they have bridges like this where you're from?"

"Of course there are bridges," I say.

"what a silly question!"

"How about that building? It's so big, you can't see the top on a cloudy day!" she says.

I turn up my nose.  Big deal.

"What about grand train stations?"

Okay, it's impressive. I'll give her that.

And this pizza is pretty tasty.

"You like bones, don't you? Look at the size of those things. They're making me drool."

Those bones are HUGE.

But come on, big bones don't make a big city.

"What about big spaces to run around
and play in?" I ask. "And big open skies?"

Like I *used* to have.

Back home.

Where everything was great.

Lulu nods. "I know just the place."

She takes off again.

We run down small alleys and squeeze past lots of humans.

It's hard to keep track of Lulu. A taxi honks right in my ear.

I yelp and twirl, and when I turn back . . .

Lulu is gone!

Suddenly, the city seems huge. A little dog like that?

She could be anywhere!

I search wide sidewalks and cross broad avenues.

I shouldn't have left my yard! The city is loud. It's bold and bright and busy . . . and *big*.

Then I smell something that reminds me of home.
Freshly cut grass! Picnic food!

I take off and run right into . . .

Lulu!

"You want big skies? Big spaces?" she asks.

"Welcome to

Central Park!"

okay, maybe this city isn't so bad.

It has big trees and big skies and big places to run.

But all you really need are big friends . . . like Lulu.

"I guess I'll fit in here after all," I say.

Lulu nudges me. "Told you so!"